A Character Building Book™

Learning About Public Service From the Life of
John F. Kennedy Jr.

Brenn Jones

The Rosen Publishing Group's
PowerKids Press™
New York

To my good friend Bradley Mark.

Published in 2002 by The Rosen Publishing Group, Inc.
29 East 21st Street, New York, NY 10010

First Edition

Book Design: Michael Caroleo

Photo Credits: p. 4 © Bettmann; Stanley Tretick, 1963/CORBIS; pp. 7, 11 © Bettmann/CORBIS; p. 8. © Ted Streshinsky/CORBIS; p. 12 © Mitchell Gerber/CORBIS; p. 15 © AP Photo/Elise Amendola; p. 16 © Reuters/Jim Bourg/Archive Photos; p. 19 © Reuters/Mike Segar/Archive Photos; p. 20 © Reuters/Peter Morgan/Archive Photos.

Jones, Brenn.
     Learning about public service from the life of John F. kennedy, Jr. / Brenn Jones.—1st ed.
       p. cm.— (A character building book)
     Includes index.
     ISBN 0-8239-5776-4 (alk. paper)
     1. Kennedy, John F. (John Fitzgerald), 1960——Juvenile literature. 2. Children of presidents—United States—Biography—Juvenile literature. [1. Kennedy, John F. (John Fitzgerald), 1960– 2. Children of presidents.] I. Title.
II. Series.
     E843.K42 J66 2002
     973.922'092—dc21   00-011698

Manufactured in the United States of America

Contents

Childhood in the White House

John Fitzgerald Kennedy Jr. was the son of John F. Kennedy, the 35th President of the United States. John was born just weeks after his father was elected president. There had not been any babies in the White House since 1893, when President Grover Cleveland's daughter was born there.

During his life, John Kennedy Jr. spent a lot of time helping other people. The use of time and energy to help other people in a community is known as public service.

◄ *As a toddler, John liked to hide under his father's desk. He also liked to play with the controls on the helicopters that landed at the White House.*

A Lasting Image

President John F. Kennedy was killed on November 22, 1963. He was 46 years old. November 25, the day of the funeral, was also John F. Kennedy Jr.'s third birthday. At the funeral, a photographer took a picture of the three-year-old saluting his father's **coffin**. The picture was in the December 6, 1963 issue of *Life* magazine. Millions of readers were moved by the image of John saluting his lost father. Throughout his life, photographers followed John around, eager to take pictures of him.

John was only three years old when his father died. This is a photograph of John at his father's funeral. ▶

Public Service

One of the things that President Kennedy did while in office was to start the Peace Corps in 1961. The Peace Corps sends people from the United States to other countries to help the people there. This kind of help is an example of public service. When he was 16, John went to Guatemala, a country in Central America, to work for the Peace Corps. There was a town in Guatemala called Rabinal that had been destroyed by an earthquake. John helped to rebuild the town.

◀ *This is President John F. Kennedy speaking at a college graduation. President Kennedy asked college students around the country to get involved in public service by joining the Peace Corps.*

Public Service Around the World

John went to college at Brown University in Providence, Rhode Island. He graduated from Brown University in 1983. During his college years, Kennedy carried on the family **tradition** of public service. In the summers between school years, he traveled to foreign countries. He worked in Kenya helping to protect the environment. He went to India in 1983 to study social work, and again in 1985 to study education and health care. After college John went to law school at New York University.

John worked as a lawyer in New York City for four years. He won all the cases that he worked on during that time. ▶

The Greatest Reward

John helped people in New York City by working with the Robin Hood **Foundation**. The Robin Hood Foundation was created in 1988. It gives money to programs that improve schools, help sick people, and give kids safe places to go after school.

In 1989, John founded Reaching Up, Inc., a nonprofit organization that helps people who work with the disabled. Reaching Up makes sure that these workers are being paid fair wages and are being well trained for their difficult jobs.

◀ *John did not just talk about public service. He acted on his beliefs as well, working to make poor and disabled peoples' lives better.*

Courage

In 1993, John and his sister Caroline decided to create an award called the Profile in Courage award. Each year the award is given to someone in politics who acts bravely and does what they know is right, even if other people try to stop them. In 2000, the award went to a woman named Hilda Solis. Solis is a **senator** in California. She has been fighting to keep California cities from putting all of their garbage dumps and pollution-causing factories in poor communities.

In 1997, the Profile in Courage award went to Judge Charles Pierce from Alabama. John, his uncle, Senator Edward Kennedy, ▶ *and his sister Caroline (behind the judge), presented the award.*

George Magazine

In 1995, John founded *George* magazine. In each issue of *George*, John interviewed people with a wide range of opinions about politics. In 1997, John and the other editors of *George* magazine wrote a book called *250 Ways to Make America Better*. This book is a collection of ideas from hundreds of different people about how to improve America. With *George* magazine, and this book, John made people think about what they could do to make the country and the world a better place.

◀ *John wanted* George *magazine to make politics more interesting to the public and to draw attention to public service.*

Secret Wedding

Magazines and newspapers were still very curious about John's personal life. John did not mind having his picture taken, but he preferred to keep his personal life private. When he got **engaged** he did not tell the press. On September 21, 1996, John secretly married Carolyn Bessette in a small wooden chapel on Cumberland Island, Georgia. Only close friends and family were invited to attend the wedding. Carolyn and John moved into an apartment in New York City.

This is a photograph of John and his wife, Carolyn Bessette Kennedy. ▶

Tragedy at Sea

In the summer of 1999, John planned to attend his cousin's wedding in Massachusetts. John had gotten his pilot's license the year before and decided to fly to the wedding. On the evening of July 16, John flew his small plane with his wife and her sister, Lauren Bessette aboard. John's plane crashed into the ocean and John, his wife Carolyn, and her sister Lauren were all killed. John F. Kennedy Jr. died at the age of 38, even younger than his father had been when he died.

After the plane crash, hundreds of people in New York City left flowers outside of Carolyn's and John's apartment.

John F. Kennedy Jr.'s Legacy

John's work in public service is still being carried out. Caroline Kennedy still gives out the Profile in Courage award every year. The Robin Hood Foundation is still helping children, and Reaching Up is still making sure that care workers are treated well on the job. *George* magazine, the magazine that John began, now presents Save The World awards for celebrities who spend time and effort on worthy causes. John devoted much of his life to helping other people. His **legacy** of public service continues to this day.

Glossary

cases (KAYS-es) A legal problem that lawyers work on.

coffin (KOH-fin) The box in which a dead person is placed for burial.

engaged (in-GAJD) Promised to be married.

foundation (fown-DAY-shun) An organization that raises and gives money to certain causes.

legacy (LEH-guh-see) Something left behind by a person's actions.

senator (SEN-uh-tor) A person who is elected to represent the people in a state.

tradition (truh-DIH-shun) A way of doing something that is passed down from one generation to the next.

Index

Web Sites

To learn more about John F. Kennedy Jr. and public service, check out these Web sites:

http://www.pj.org/people/jfk0720.cfm

http://www.who2.com/johnfkennedyjr.html